Ponyella

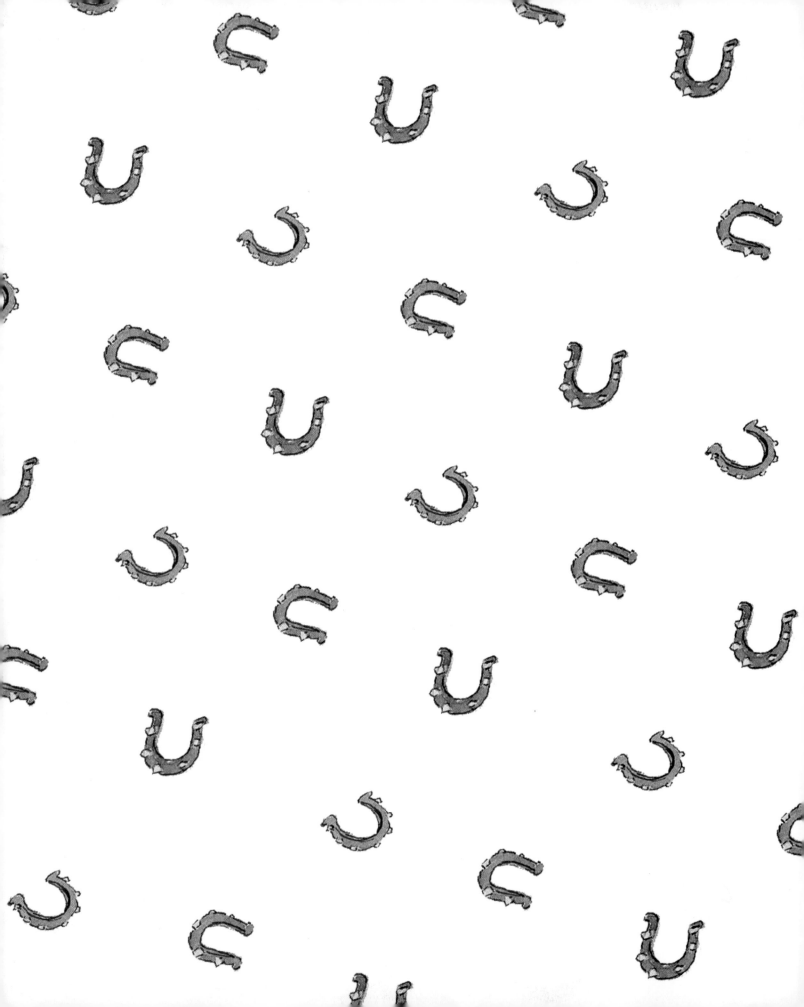

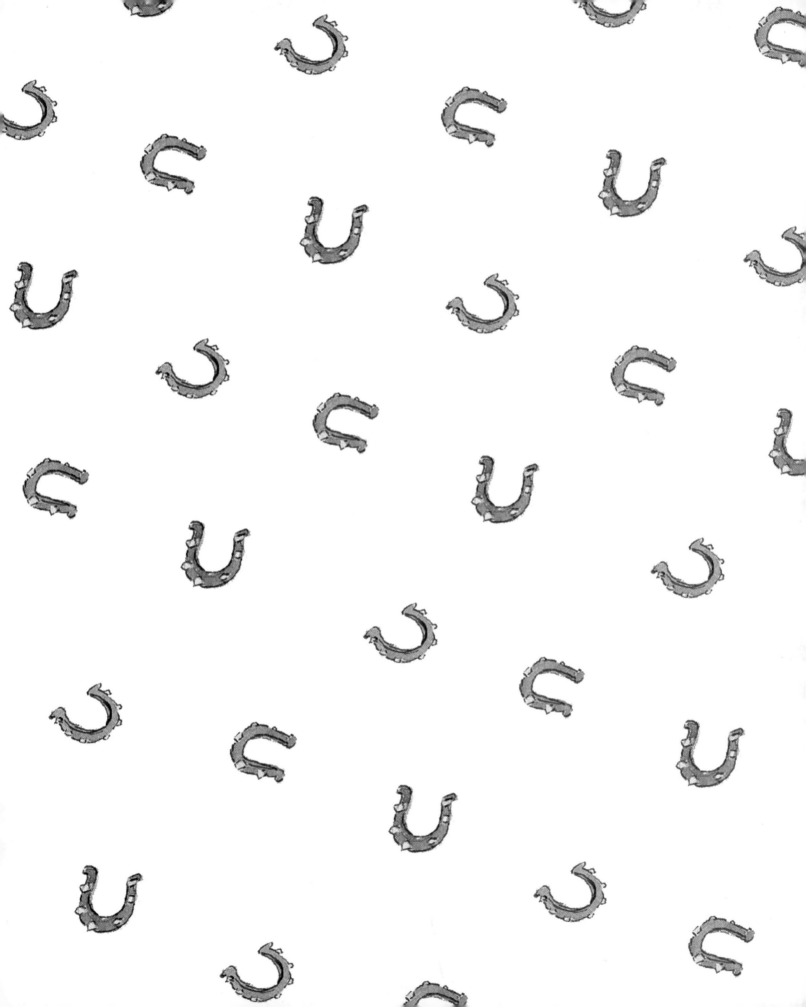

For anyone who's ever wanted a pony.
—L.N.

For my wonderful nieces and nephews:
Whitney and Jessie,
Chloe,
Mykayla, Jamie, John, Zack, and Brendan;
May each of you discover your own "happily ever after"
—N.E.

For Nikki
—L.M.

ISBN 978-0-545-48220-2

Text copyright © 2011 by Laura Numeroff and Nate Evans.
Illustrations copyright © 2011 by Lynn Munsinger.
All rights reserved. Published by Scholastic Inc., 557 Broadway, New York, NY 10012,
by arrangement with Hyperion Books for Children, an imprint of Disney Book Group, LLC.
SCHOLASTIC and associated logos are trademarks and/or registered trademarks of Scholastic Inc.

12 11 10 9 8 7 6 5 4 3 2 1   12 13 14 15 16 17/0

Printed in the U.S.A.   40

This edition first printing, September 2012

Ponyella

Laura Numeroff and Nate Evans
pictures by Lynn Munsinger

SCHOLASTIC INC.
New York Toronto London Auckland
Sydney Mexico City New Delhi Hong Kong

Once upon a time there was a beautiful horse named Ponyella.
Her coat was white as marshmallow, and her mane was long and silky.
She lived on a small farm with green pastures and a lovely barn.
Ponyella was very happy.

One day she was having fun jumping when she noticed a sign on the front gate.

Soon Ponyella's owners were driving away, and new people were moving in.
They brought their two ponies, Plumpkin and Bun Bun.
"This place is hideous," said Plumpkin.

"I can't believe we have to live with *her*," Bun Bun said, glaring at Ponyella.

"My coat is much prettier than hers," said Plumpkin. "White is so boring!"

"And my mane is much nicer than hers," snorted Bun Bun jealously. "She looks like she's wearing a clown wig!"

Plumpkin and Bun Bun did not like Ponyella one bit.

They made such a fuss that the new owner put Ponyella in a tiny, smelly stall that was way out in the back.

She never got to jump anymore.

When Ponyella wasn't pulling a coal-filled cart, she was tied up.
Her coat became as gray as a rain cloud.
Ponyella was miserable.
Even Sam, the barn mouse, felt sorry for her.

One day a big shiny car drove by. There was a little girl with red hair and freckles in the backseat.

"That's Princess Penelope!" said Bun Bun. "I heard that she lives on a magnificent royal ranch."

"I wish I could live with her," said Plumpkin. "I'd have carrot cake every day!"

The princess looks so kind, thought Ponyella, pulling her heavy cart.

"Well, I heard Princess Penelope's going to pick the winner of the Tippington 25th Annual Grand Royal Pony Championship!" said Bun Bun. "It's the most important pony show of the year, and I'm sure *I'll* win!"

"No, I will!" said Plumpkin.

"When is the show?" Ponyella asked excitedly.

"What does it matter?" Bun Bun sneered. "You're not going!"

"You're dirty and ugly and smell like a pig," said Plumpkin. "Oink, oink!"

On the day of the show, grooms readied Bun Bun and Plumpkin, then drove them away in a fancy horse trailer.

Ponyella began to cry.

Suddenly there was a puff of smoke and a spray of sparkles!

POOF!
An old mare wearing a cape appeared.

"Who are you?" asked Ponyella.

"I am your fairy godmare," said the horse. "Why are you crying?"

"I want to go to the Tippington 25th Annual Grand Royal Pony Championship," Ponyella said.

"Then you shall go," the fairy godmare said. "Fetch me a big, juicy apple."

All Ponyella could find was an old apple core.

"Close enough," said the fairy godmare.

She swished her tail and . . .

POOF!
There was a trailer!

"Now we need someone to drive the trailer," the fairy godmare said.

"I can do it!" cried Sam.

The fairy godmare wiggled her ears and . . .

POOF!
Sam turned into a driver.

"Cheese Louise!" said Sam.
Then the fairy godmare swished her tail again and . . .

POOF!
Ponyella looked absolutely beautiful!

And most magically of all,
Ponyella had sparkling diamond horseshoes!

As Ponyella got into the trailer, her fairy godmare said, "Now remember, you must be home by the stroke of noon. That's when everything returns to normal, and you'll look exactly as you did before!"

Ponyella arrived at the show.
When she walked past Bun Bun and Plumpkin, they didn't even recognize her.
"Isn't that the fancy pony from Paris?" whispered Bun Bun.
"You're right," said Plumpkin. "It's Fifi la Frou-Frou!"

Soon it was time for the championship event.

Several ponies took their turn going over the jumps, but none of them could make it over the last one. It was too high.

Then it was Bun Bun's turn. She missed almost every jump!

When it was time for Plumpkin, she knocked all the jumps over!

Finally Ponyella trotted into the ring.

She got over the first jump just fine.

The second and third jumps were trickier, but she made them, too.

All she had to do was make it over that last jump.

Ponyella jumped up, up, up . . .
and over she went!
The crowd cheered.
"Where did that amazing pony come from?" someone yelled.
It was Princess Penelope.

All of a sudden the clock struck twelve.
"Oh no!" cried Sam. "Don't forget what that old horse said!"
Ponyella galloped toward her trailer so fast, she lost a shoe!
"Wait!" called the princess.
But Ponyella couldn't wait.

Ponyella and Sam hurried home. Halfway there . . .

POOF!
Everything turned back to the way it was.

Ponyella ran home as fast as she could, Sam clinging desperately to her mane.

Later that afternoon, Bun Bun and Plumpkin returned from the show.

"Did the princess pick a champion?" Ponyella asked.

"Not yet," said Plumpkin. "But I'm sure it's me!"

"No, I was the best!" Bun Bun said.

"Put a muzzle on it," said Plumpkin.

"Go eat an apple with a worm in it!" said Bun Bun, and the two fought all night about which of them would win.

The next morning, Princess Penelope arrived at the ranch.

"I'm looking for the champion," said the princess. "Whoever this diamond horseshoe fits is the winner!"

Plumpkin and Bun Bun rushed over to see if the horseshoe fit.

Bun Bun tried wiggling her foot, but it was too skinny.

Plumpkin tried stomping her foot into the shoe, but her hoof was too pudgy.

"Oh no," said the princess sadly. "I'm never going to find my champion pony!"

Ponyella pulled frantically at her rope, but she couldn't get free.

"I'll help you!" said Sam, and he chewed through the rope.

Ponyella ran toward the princess.

Plumpkin and Bun Bun tried to trip her, but Ponyella jumped right over them.

"Holy haystacks, what a jump!" cried the princess. "Stop the car!"

She took the diamond horseshoe and tried it on Ponyella.
It fit perfectly!
Plumpkin and Bun Bun fainted.

"Someone needs a bath," the princess said. Then she nuzzled Ponyella's nose.

"I want you to be my pony," the princess whispered. "I'm going to buy you, no matter what it costs!"

The princess gave Ponyella's owner a big piggy bank filled with all the allowance she had saved.

The princess took Ponyella home and threw her a fabulous bridle party.
She brushed Ponyella every day and fed her carrot muffins.
Ponyella had the roomiest stall she'd ever seen.
"Boy, this is the life!" said Sam.

Ponyella jumped all the time, and she lived happily ever after.

As for Plumpkin and Bun Bun, they were sold to a new owner.
But that's another story.

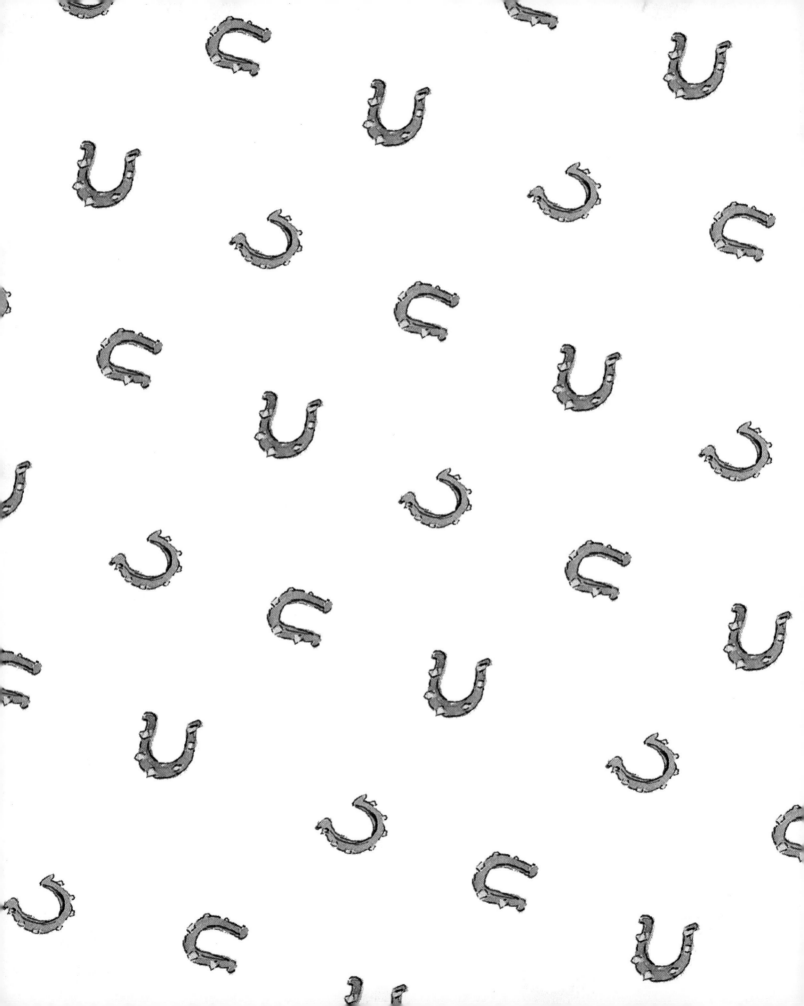